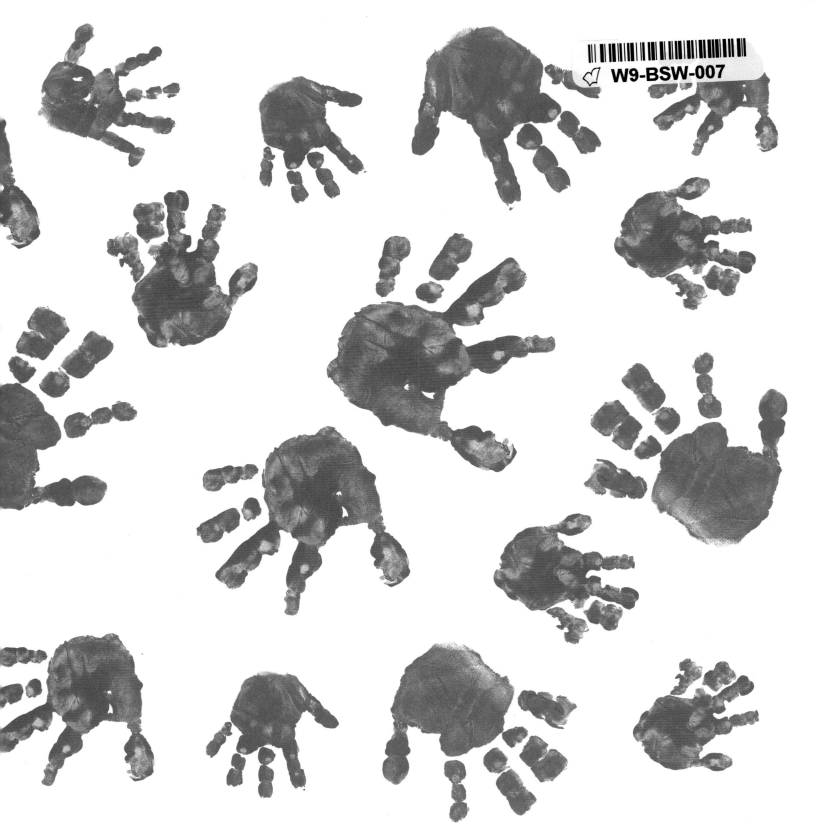

The Making of My Special Hand

Dedicated to the memory of Dr. Robert Keagy, orthopedic surgeon, clinic chief of the
children's amputee program at the Rehabilitation Institute of Chicago (RIC), 1959-1997,
and a special friend to many families and professionals of the amputee program at RIC.

Special Thanks
To the Variety Club/Ann and Jack Sparberg's
Children's Amputee Program of Illinois for financial support
To Dr. Don Olson for the patience, laughter, and guidance he shared with me in the development of this book
To Steve Duff, assistant prosthetist, who assisted in the development of this book
To the professional staff of the children's amputee program at RIC
To Stephanie, Greg, Scott, and Madison Reed for graciously allowing me
to share an important time in their lives with readers everywhere
To my husband, Bobby, and our children, Dominic, Grant, and Gianna,
for encouraging me to use my skills to educate others about disabilities. I love you all!

—J.R.H.

Published by
PEACHTREE PUBLISHERS, LTD.
1700 Chattahoochee Avenue
Atlanta, GA 30318-2112

©1998 by the Rehabilitation Institute of Chicago

Book design by Nicola Simmonds and Matthew Carmack
Original photography by Jamee Riggio Heelan
Printed in Singapore
10 9 8 7 6 5 4 3

Library of Congress Cataloging-in-Publication Data
Heelan, Jamee Riggio
    The making of my special hand : Madison's Story / Jamee Riggio Heelan ; illustrations by Nicola
Simmonds Carter.
        p. cm. – (A Rehabilitation Institute of Chicago learning book)
       Summary: A child who was born with one hand tells the story of how people at the hospital made
a helper hand for her, how the new hand operates, how it feels, and how she can use it.
    ISBN 1-56145-186-X
    1. Artificial hands—Juvenile literature. 2. Physically handicapped children—Rehabilitation—Juvenile
literature. [1.Artificial hands. 2. Physically handicapped.] I. Carter, Nicola Simmonds, ill. II. Title. III.
Series.
RD756.22.H44 1998
617.5'7503—dc21
                                            98-18086
                                            CIP
                                            AC

A Rehabilitation Institute of Chicago Learning Book

The Making of My Special Hand
Madison's Story

Jamee Riggio Heelan, OTR/L
Rehabilitation Institute of Chicago

Illustrations by Nicola Simmonds

PEACHTREE
ATLANTA

Hi, my name is Madison. I was born with one hand. I want to tell you a story about how I got my helper hand. And you will see how much T.L.C. (tender loving care) went into the making of a very special part of me, my new hand.

My family and I visited a hospital that has a Children's Amputee Program. First we saw Jamee, an occupational therapist. She told us all about helper hands. We got to touch them and see how they work. Here are some she showed us:

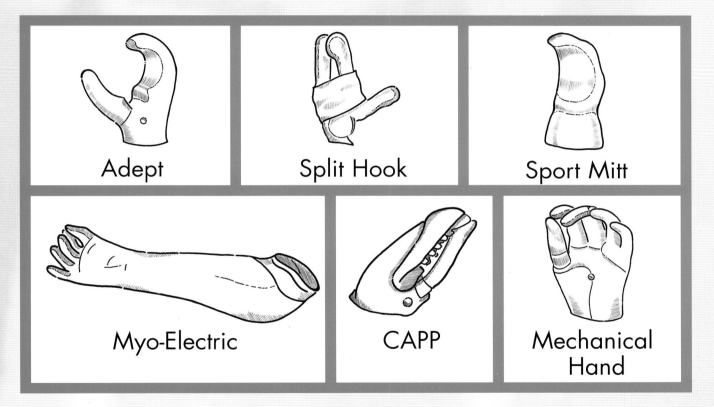

Adept

Split Hook

Sport Mitt

Myo-Electric

CAPP

Mechanical Hand

She said she would teach me how my special hand works, how to take care of it, and how to use it while I play.

Jamee called the doctor, who came to look at my arm. The doctor told me I was ready to have a helper hand. My parents and my new friends at the hospital chose the myo-electric helper hand for me. They called it a myo-electric prosthesis. "Myo" means muscle and "prosthesis" is a fancy word for helper hand.
With my own muscle movements and a battery, my new hand will open and close.

Next we visited Jack, the prosthetist. He is the person who made my hand. He told my mom and me how helper hands are made.

Jack put on funny rubber gloves and drew lines all over my arm with a marker.

He rubbed my arm with gel, so the plaster would not stick to my skin. It tickled and made me giggle.

Then he put wet plaster on my arm. Around and around my arm it went. It felt slimy and cold. It got warm as it began to harden.

We waited a few minutes for the plaster cast to harden, and Jack slid the cast off my arm.

Now the hardest part was over!

Then Jack measured both arms to make sure my helper hand and my other arm were the same length.

Then I went home. While I was gone, my new friends were busy making my special hand.

And this is how it was done.

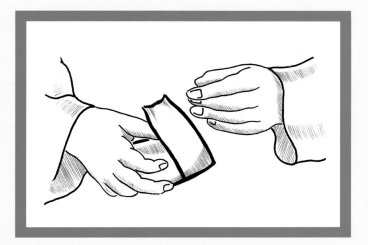

Jack put tape on the open part of my cast.

Then he sprayed the inside with something slippery.

He mixed
some plaster

and poured it
into my cast.

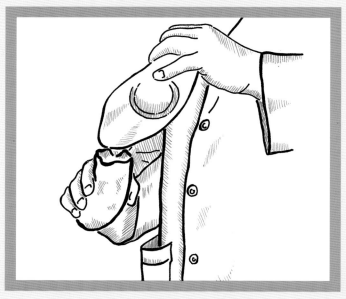

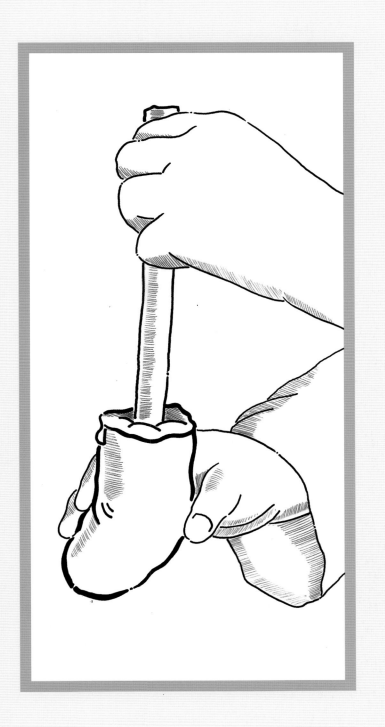

He put a piece of
pipe in the wet plaster.
It was like a handle.
Then he let the
plaster harden.

After the plaster
hardened, Jack added
more plaster
to smooth out my cast.

Then he shaped
the cast with a tool
to look just
like my arm.

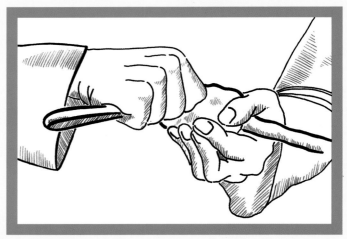

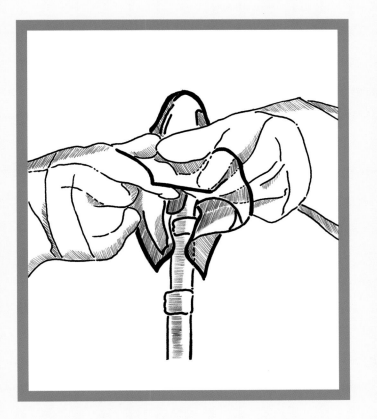

Next he put hot plastic over the plaster cast of my arm. The plastic formed to the shape of my arm and created a socket. When the plastic socket hardened, the cast was removed. The socket fit onto my arm and helped hold my helper hand to my arm.

During my second visit to the hospital, Jamee took us to see Jack.
He put the socket onto my arm to make sure it fit. And he let me play with the cloth that he used to help pull the socket on my arm.

He cut an opening in the plastic socket for an electrode, which sends a signal to my hand to make the hand move.

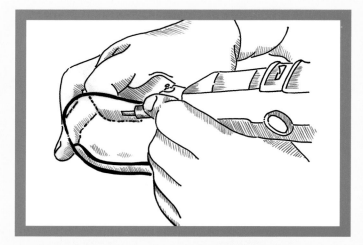

Then he connected the battery.

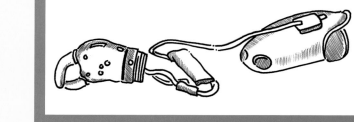

Jack taped together these three pieces—the socket, the battery, and my helper hand —for me to try.

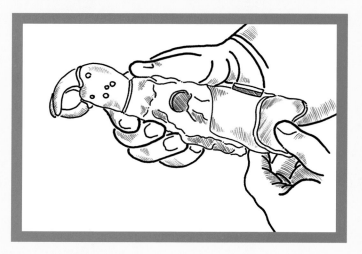

He told me how the hand fit, and before my eyes
he slipped it on my arm.

It was very easy to put on.
A small switch in the socket turned on
the battery to make it work.

It did not hurt at all.
It looked a little different from my
other hand, but I liked it.

Look at that! When I moved my muscle, the fingers opened!

I took my helper hand to Jamee in the Occupational Therapy Department where I jumped and tumbled. We made sure the helper hand was able to stay on.

During my second visit, Jamee taught me how to use my hand while I played.

Look, I tumbled and it did not fall off!
I gave my hand back to my new friends so they
could finish it. Then my mom and I went home.
I looked forward to my next visit when I would
get to take my special hand home with me.

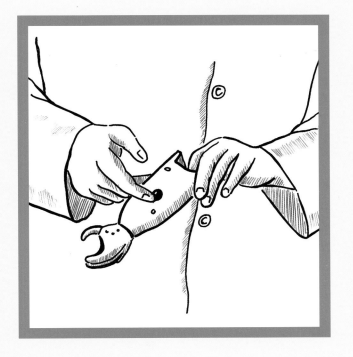

Our third visit to the hospital was my special day. Jack showed my mom how to turn the hand on and off, and how to charge the battery at night. If the battery is not charged, my hand will not work.

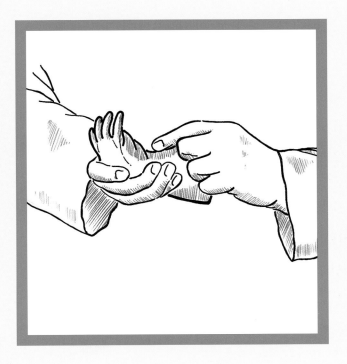

Then he showed her how to put on the glove. It protects my helper hand and makes it look like my other hand.

I learned a lot about my helper
hand. Moving my muscle opens
the hand, and it can pinch
like a real hand.
OUCH!
At first I was a little scared
to use my new hand, but then
I began to really like it.
I discovered all the fun things
I could do with it.
I could pick up toys, throw a ball,
and I could carry things. When I get
bigger, I will need a new one,
the way my growing feet
will need new shoes.

I love my special hand. I can wear it as long as I want and any time I want. It's part of me now. Thank you for letting me share my story.
Love, Madison